HENRY
and the Red Stripes

Story and Pictures by
**Eileen
Christelow**

CLARION BOOKS
TICKNOR & FIELDS : A HOUGHTON MIFFLIN COMPANY
NEW YORK

One day, Henry Rabbit painted a picture
of a mother, a father, and a little boy rabbit.
He colored them brown with red stripes.
    His friend Max painted a picture of a flower.

Henry showed his picture to his father.
His father said, "That's a wonderful painting,
but rabbits are brown all over—the color of
dry leaves. Rabbits don't have stripes."
"They can if they want to," said Henry.

He showed his picture to his mother.
"What a lovely picture!" she said. "But rabbits
are brown all over—the color of twigs and bark.
Rabbits don't have stripes."

"They can if they want to!" said Henry.

Henry went back to his paints.
He painted red stripes on himself.

Max helped him.

"You look silly!" Max said.
"I know!" giggled Henry.

Henry and Max raced through the woods. They skipped

and they danced, and Henry showed off his new red stripes.

Suddenly they stopped.

"A fox!" squealed Max, darting under a rock.

"Quiet!" whispered Henry, scrambling into a thicket of twigs and dry leaves. "Don't move! The fox will never see you."

But Henry forgot about his bright red stripes.

"I've got you!" cried the fox.
"Help!" shrieked Henry, and he tried to run.

But the fox grabbed him, and stuffed him in a sack.
"Rabbit stew!" drooled the hungry fox as he
hurried home with Henry slung over his shoulder.
Max hurried in the opposite direction, to tell
Henry's parents the bad news.

"What a strange looking rabbit!" exclaimed Mrs. Fox when she opened the sack. "Why does he have red stripes?"

"All rabbits should have red stripes," said Mr. Fox. "It makes them easier to see!"

Mrs. Fox examined Henry skeptically as she waited for the water in the stew pot to boil.

"Perhaps he has a terrible disease," she worried.

"Nonsense," said Mr. Fox.

"If we eat him, we might get sick too!"

"Nonsense!" yelled Mr. Fox, sprinkling Henry with pepper.

"Perhaps an evil spell was cast on him!"
said Mrs. Fox.

"That's more nonsense!" said Mr. Fox.

"I won't cook this rabbit!" shouted
Mrs. Fox, stamping her foot.

"Well, I will!" roared Mr. Fox.

"Aah—aah—aah—choo!" sneezed Henry.

Henry spluttered and wheezed and trembled and crossed his eyes and made a ghastly face.

Mrs. Fox shrieked, "I told you! Something is wrong with that rabbit!"

She quickly stuffed Henry back into the canvas sack and hurled it out the door.

"That's my dinner!" yelled Mr. Fox, running after the sack.

But Henry was already half way home.

"We thought we'd never see you again," cried his worried parents. "Max told us what happened!"

They hugged Henry...

and scolded him,

and kissed him,

and scrubbed him until the red stripes were washed away.

Sometimes Henry still likes
to wear red stripes...

...in the house. But when he is outside,

he wears his plain brown fur, which is
the color of dry leaves, twigs and bark.